Walter Finds a Home

By Cat Smith with Brad & Kelly Blake

Illustrations by JASMINE "JAZZY" SMITH

Archway Publishing books may be ordered through booksellers or by contacting:

Archway Publishing
1663 Liberty Drive
Bloomington, IN 47403
www.archwaypublishing.com
844.669.3957

"Walter Finds A Home" by Cat Smith with Brad and Kelly Blake
And introducing Walter, the Orphaned Donkey.

ISBN: 978-1-4808-9615-4 (sc)
ISBN: 978-1-4808-9616-1 (e)

Print information available on the last page.

Archway Publishing rev. date: 10/08/2020

Walter

Dedicated to Walter and all the burros that call Oatman home.

Brad
Kelly

It was a chilly summer night in the Arizona desert. The moon shined high in the sky. The coyotes howled and the owls hooted.

Except one animal who
was alone and scared.

It was a newborn donkey who was lying down in the dirt crying. He needed his mama, but couldn't find her. He wondered where she was.

The little donkey tried to stand up, but he couldn't. His legs were too wobbly, he fell to the ground and began to cry. His mama was not there to teach him to walk or to feed him. She was not there to keep him warm. Where was his mama?

The donkey began to cry again.

Only this time a funny noise came out of the donkey's mouth.

"Hee haw! Hee haw!" said the donkey.

The sound scared the little donkey. It scared the birds and all the animals that were around him in the desert.

It even scared Mr. Snake, who didn't look so friendly.

The donkey walked around until he became very hungry and sleepy. He was also very, very thirsty. He kept walking until he found a small stream of water, running down the mountain.

He walked over and put his face close to the water. He could see his face. It scared him! Even his big, floppy ears scared him! He quickly ran away from the water. His legs were not wobbly anymore.

When the donkey felt safe, he laid down on the desert ground and began to fall asleep. Suddenly, the donkey awoke to a loud noise.

"BANG!"

It was the sound of a truck door being closed and when he opened his eyes, he saw a man and woman standing near him.

The donkey began to bray again, "Hee haw! Hee haw!"

What the donkey didn't know was they were there to rescue him. To take him home and make him part of their family.

The man and woman, whose names were Brad and Kelly, had heard about a lonely donkey needing help after its mama left him all alone.

The donkey didn't know his mama was very young herself when he was born and she couldn't care for him.

The donkey could see that Brad and Kelly were very friendly. Brad reached his hand out to the donkey and when the donkey sniffed it, Brad gently placed a blanket around him and picked him up.

Brad and Kelly brought the donkey home and began to care for him. They cuddled him and gave him a bottle of milk. It was good and filled his tummy. He wasn't hungry or scared anymore.

The donkey was happy. He played with four dogs that lived at the house with him. They even went on walks in the desert as a family.

One night while Brad was in the living room feeding the donkey his bottle, Kelly walked in and told him she thought of a name...WALTER!

The next few days were busy for all of them. Brad and Kelly worked together with other people to help adopt Walter.

Weeks later, Walter was adopted. He was now part of Brad and Kelly's family.

Walter had found his forever family.
Even if they did look different from him.

If you are interested in adopting a wild burro, donkey or mustang, contact your local Bureau of Land Management Field Office (BLM) to inquire about their program.

Please remember that the wildlife residing in the Oatman desert are part of the community. Removal of an animal is protected by federal laws.

ABOUT THE AUTHORS

Cat is an awarding-winning journalist who resides in Arizona with her young daughter, Brooklyn. In her downtime when she isn't writing, Cat likes to watch her daughter's baseball games, hang out at the river and lake, catch a movie at the local theater, travel to the mountains, volunteer with organizations within her community and enjoy family time with her mom, Anne Z. Smith, on their ranch.

The Blake's reside in Oatman, Arizona, an old western mining town that dates back to 1903 and has burros roaming freely in town. The two met when they were eight-years-old when their families became friends. The Blake's are high school sweethearts. They married in 2009 and own several family businesses in Oatman. Their love for animals is another big part of their lives. They couldn't imagine not having Walter or their four German Shepard's as their family members. They have a lot of help taking care of their animal village from their parents and other family members.